MW00604360

Rita and the Firefighters

To Kerri Meyer, who believes in all children
—Mike Huber

To my little guy, Phoenix,
whose imagination and energy are a constant inspiration
—Joseph Cowman

Published by Redleaf Lane
An imprint of Redleaf Press
10 Yorkton Court
Saint Paul, MN 55117
www.RedleafLane.org

First edition 2014
Book jacket and interior page design by Jim Handrigan
Main body text set in Billy
Typeface provided by MyFonts

Manufactured in Canada
20 19 18 17 16 15 14 13 1 2 3 4 5 6 7 8

Library of Congress Control Number: 2013939328

Rita watched the firefighters walk back to the fire station. She watched them type at their computers—tkk-tah-tkk-tkk.

"Can I play?" she asked. But Jayden and Michi didn't hear her.

“Ring-ring!” Michi picked up the phone. “Fire station . . .
Oh no! A fire? At the ice cream shop? We’ll be right there!”

Michi and Jayden scrambled to put out the fire.

Back at the firehouse, Michi said, “That was a big fire. We need to write a big report.” Michi and Jayden went to work. Tkk-tah-tkk-tkk.

Rita was just about to ask, “Can I play?” when the firehouse phone rang again.

"Another fire!" Jayden yelled. The firefighters grabbed their gear.

Rita decided to step in their way.
“Can I play too?” she asked again.

But Jayden and Michi scooted around her.
"No," Michi said. "We have to put out the fire."

Rita was feeling left out.

Johanna put down her book and asked Rita, “Do you want to play firefighter too?”

Rita said, “I want to play. I don’t want to be a firefighter. I want to be a kitty.”

Johanna said, "But Michi and Jayden are playing firefighter. You still want to play with them?"

"They're having fun," said Rita. "I want to play."

"Okay," said Johanna. "Come on, kitty. Let's go see the firefighters."

Johanna held Rita's hand. She said to Michi and Jayden, "I have been taking care of this kitty, but I have to go to work now. Can she take a nap in your fire truck?"

Michi said, “We need a fire truck!” He grabbed two chairs and set them side by side. Jayden made a cat bed behind the chairs using blocks.

Rita lay down, and Johanna covered her up. “Good-bye, kitty,” she said. “I’m going to work.”

There was another “ring-ring!” and Jayden picked up the phone. “Michi! Another fire! Let’s go!”

But Michi put his finger to his lips. “Shhh. The kitty’s sleeping.” He patted the kitty gently.

Purr

Jayden brought over the clipboards and handed one to Michi. "Maybe we could write our fire reports on paper so we don't wake the kitty." The firefighters both started writing.

While they were working, Rita crept out of bed.
Michi noticed and said, “Come back, kitty!”

He hurried after her, but she crawled under the table.
"Jayden!" Michi said. "Help me catch the kitty!"

Michi and Jayden took Rita by the paws and led her back to the fire truck. But as soon as the firefighters started working, the kitty was off again.

The firefighters laughed as they barreled after her. Rita smiled. She knew playing with Michi and Jayden would be fun.

A Note to Readers

Joining play that's already under way can be hard for some children. Rita wants to join Jayden and Michi, but she doesn't know how. Sometimes adults forget that joining play requires some fairly sophisticated skills. Children need to read body language accurately. They must listen to figure out what the others are playing. Finally, they must play a role that fits the situation, talking to the others in that role and addressing them in their own particular roles. It takes time and practice to learn these skills.

You can help by modeling behaviors children can use to enter play. One of the best ways to help young children who are having trouble entering play is to act as a playmate and to demonstrate how to join in. In *Rita and the Firefighters*, for example, Johanna helps Rita ease into the boys' play by asking if the kitty can take a nap in their fire truck. Johanna creates a role for Rita that works within the context of the firefighter play, and then Rita joins in.

We hope *Rita and the Firefighters* helps children consider the different ways they can join the play going on around them.

Written by
MIKE HUBER

Illustrated by
JOSEPH COWMAN

Red Leaf
Lane

Rita watched Jayden and Michi race by.
The firefighters were on their way!

She could tell they were having fun.
She wanted to have fun too.